THE
ADVENTURES OF
DUCK

ISBN 978-1-63814-145-7 (Paperback)
ISBN 978-1-63814-146-4 (Digital)

Covenant Books, Inc.
11661 Hwy 707
Murrells Inlet, SC 29576
www.covenantbooks.com

THE ADVENTURES OF DUCK

Shayla McGowan

1

The sun was rising over the cattails in Mr. McGruber's pond when Duck heard his friend Sally the bullfrog let out a big CROAK.

He would wake up every morning to the sound of Sally greeting the sun with her loud, booming chirp, and once awake, it was time to get ready for the day. Duck would stretch his neck as far as it would go and shake his tail feathers so fast all his loose feathers would fly off; then he would wait patiently for Mr. McGruber to open the gate so that he could go outside.

Duck lived in Mr. McGruber's big yellow barn, and he loved his little home. Along with an entire barn to himself, Duck also had his very own pond!

One of his favorite things to do was to swim around the edges of Mr. McGruber's pond and find tiny bugs to eat for a snack. Bugs were okay to eat for a snack, but Duck's favorite thing to eat was bread, and Mr. McGruber always made sure to share with him.

There was also another very special place that Duck loved, a willow tree right next to Mr. McGruber's pond, and it was the perfect place to sit for some shade on hot summer days.

Duck loved his pond and his willow tree, but every day, he would take a stroll around his yard and visit his other friends. He had all kinds of friends: Sara the sparrow, Pip the chipmunk, Max the hummingbird, Bobby the raccoon, and so many others.

On his walk, he would always make time to stop and have lunch with Sara and Pip at the bird feeders. Sometimes he would even visit Mr. McGruber's neighbors on his daily walks.

When the sun began to set and his friends all went home,

Duck would make his way back to his barn to get ready for bedtime.

Mr. McGruber would open the gate,

and Duck would waddle into his comfy, warm bed to get tucked in for the night

and dream of what kind of adventures he would have the next day.

About the Author

Shayla McGowan is from a small country town in Ohio. She loves living in the country but visits the beach every chance she gets, particularly the Outer Banks, North Carolina. She has always loved animals and has had many pets over the years, including ducks. She has her bachelor's degree in psychology and loves her job, working in health care. She also loves being involved in her church and is very close to her family. Shayla hopes that this book brings as much joy to you as it has to her.